Between Two Hearts

A book of poetry between a lost grandmother
& the love of a granddaughter

Tammy Crawford and co-written by Lillie M. Byers Lueck

authorHOUSE

AuthorHouse™
1663 Liberty Drive
Bloomington, IN 47403
www.authorhouse.com
Phone: 833-262-8899

Published by AuthorHouse 12/28/2022

ISBN: 978-1-4389-3328-3 (sc)

Print information available on the last page.

This book is printed on acid-free paper.

Only a moment of time shall separate our distance

Dedication

This book of poetry is dedicated in loving memory, to my Grandmother, Lillie M. Byers Lueck.

1916-1987

I wanted to do something to honor my late grandmother. I came across a notebook of poetry she had written on some blank pages, and knew I wanted to have her as my co-writer. Our styles of writing are very different from one another, but we still have a story to tell. As with a song, a poem can tell a story in just a few short lines. This is for you grandma!

Contents

Bluebird's Valentine

A boy bluebird was very sad,
For he had no wife to make him glad.
He would not sing, he would not fly,
But would sit in our apple tree and sigh.

Soon another bluebird came fly by.
Then said the first bird, "My, oh my!"
Oh, if that bird were only mine,
I'd marry her for my Valentine!

One day he heard her singing,
"Oh, I would happy be…
If that gay feathered bird in the apple tree,
Would only ask to marry me."

So he married her, that gay blue bird,
And now his singing can be heard.
They built their home in our apple tree,
And were happy with their babies three.
And the bluebird sang,
"She's mine; I've got her now for my Valentine!"

By the Sea

Down by the sea shore
As the sun sets low,
I sit on the beachfront
Watching the sun's fading glow.

You told me, this is where I'd find you,
If ever I was in need.
To feel your love around me,
This is the place it would be.

I come here daily, but never are you here,
I reach up and wipe yet, another weary tear.
Memories surround me as I wait patiently,
You will be here today I have to believe.

I will come again tomorrow,
I'll wait by the sea,
As waves crash in around me,
I will drift off to sleep.

As I awoke from my dream,
With a peace I have never known,
I looked up to find you with a heavenly glow.
Reaching out to take my hand, you finally lead me home.

My Love

When you look at me with your eyes,
I want so much to believe your alibis.
You have hurt me more that I could take,
now I live with an unbearable heartache.
You took from me so very much,
How to believe, love, trust, and such.
I have closed my eyes and given up.
There is nothing left to bring me up.
Will I ever trust again?
Will I ever be free to begin?
The pain grips and holds on tight,
never leaving, day, or night.
You never played fair or for keeps,
you threw away the best part of me.
Now I often wonder why,
there ever were a you and I.
If I could turn back time and start again,
would I be able to, knowing how it would end.
If I knew then what I know now,
I would have just stayed friends.

Springtime

There was a little bird,
That sat up in the tree.
He sang and sang,
A beautiful song to me.

I loved this little bird,
I played and played with him.
Then his little wife came,
And they built a home on a limb.

Then she laid some eggs,
And had some little birds.
Those cunning little things,
They were too sweet for words.

They sang around the town,
Where the butterflies did fly.
I loved to watch them all,
Sailing in the blue, blue sky.

Take My Hand

Take my hand and walk with me
on down by the moonlit sea.
We can sit together on the sand so pure
and remind each other of our love so sure.

Take my hand and walk with me
and let us remember our yesterdays
when we were young and not so old,
Let us be young again and a little bold.

Take my hand and walk with me.
I know you have forgotten from time to time.
I know how Alzheimer's has erased your mind,
and now we have so little of time.

Take my hand and walk with me.
Give me one more day for you and me.
Give me strength to carry on, for tomorrow,
my love, you may be gone.

Flowers all around me

Flowers all around me,
Blossoming in the sun,
Makes me shiver with delight,
Makes me smile so very bright.

Spread your petals on the ground,
Let them shimmer all around,
May they brighten up my day?
So that I may smile, come what may.

I feel their softness on my face,
I take pleasure with each embrace.
May I lie in their bed of petals?
Their softness like the wings of Angels.

Such many colors of rare pure beauty,
As they sway in time, as if in courting.
I linger on as time drifts by,
Thanking God for all, in His home up high.

Three Riddles in Rhyme

A piece of wood, which must be good,
And stand much strain, I'm sure.
Folks play with me and always try,
To make a good high score.
You will also find I am on the wing
When the sun low, does sink.
Yet tho I fly and rise so high, I am no bird,
So think and see if you can find my name.
You'll find me used in a national game.
Something, nothing, as you use me.
Small or bulky, as you choose me.
Fat and round, just like a boy,
Always present when there's joy.
Eternity I bring to view,
The sun and all the planets too.
You'll never find an end to me,
And all the world resembles me.
I know a word of plural number,
A foe to all, peace, and slumber.
Most any word you may take,
By adding "s" the plural, you make.
But if you add an "s" to this,
Behold the metamorphosis.
Plural is the word now no more,
And sweet what was bitter before.

The Meadow Lark

As I was walking in the field one day,
I saw a little meadow lark at play.
He said, "I will sing to you my friend,
If to me your ear you'll lend."

I gave him some crumbs to eat,
Also some seeds and a bit of fat meat.
"Thank you," he chirped, with a voice full of cheer,
"I'll see you later on in the year."

He flew to the fence post
And trilled a sweet note.
My dear little friend,
With his neat feather coat.

Please Remember Us

The doom of forbidding grips my heart so very tight.
I cannot believe I am down here, where I can see not even light.
Where it came from, no one even knows,
not any air to breath, my lungs tell me this is so.
Help should be coming; it is in the training we have had.
I can wait it out; it should not be too bad.
My pals are down here with me,
a prayer is what's in need.
For we really want to believe,
that no one will have to grieve.
Have our families even been notified?
Even now, do they wait outside?
I can feel a rumble,
and the shifting all around.
Please do not send us any farther,
underneath this darkened ground.
Please, will you find us soon, before we write our last good-byes,
to our loved ones, we would forever be leaving behind.
Our time is drawing nearer as the hours go on by;
I have now even lost my strength, I do not even want to cry.
I have made my peace with God,
Should He now even call me home.
Surrounded by the Angels,
We know we are not alone.
They call us miners, and our work is underground
please remember us, for we may never be found.

Grandma's poem

Untiltled

If you strike a thorn or rose,
Keep a – goin'.
If it hails or if it snows,
Keep a – goin'.
Taint no use to sit and whine,
When the fish aint on your line;
Bait your hook an' keep on tryin',
Keep a – goin'.
Blank cartridge, big gun,
All talk, little done.

Grandma's poem

The Eyes

Eyes that are always telling lies,
Naughty eyes.
Eyes that are blue or gray,
Whoa, what do you want to make eyes at me for,
At you for? Just to steal your heart away.
Eyes like a bull dog, very wise wicked eyes.
Eyes that look you through,
But of all the eyes I've seen,
Only two look good to me
And there the eyes that say, "I love you."

I Promised

I promised, one day I would give you a ring,
One that sparkled of diamonds and gold
That would always make your heart sing.
Look in the chest, at the end of the bed,
How beautiful it is, a sight to behold.
Go ahead my love; put it on your finger.
I don't mind let your eyes linger.
I promised, one day I would make you my wife,
And that we would have a wonderful life.
Look love, in the bottom of my dresser,
See them, the invitations, all bound in leather.
We were ready to mail them, for our friends to see,
But we didn't make it, for I was sent to serve our country.
I promised, one day I would buy you a home,
One you would be proud of, with plenty of rooms to roam.
Look love, in the glove box of my car.
Keys to unlock the door. Go around the corner, down the street,
You see the one, wasn't I pretty discrete?
Go ahead unlock the door, take a peek inside.
I was going to bring you here as my new bride.
I promised, one day, I would sing you a song,
Now my voice is so sure and strong.
The song I give to you is, "I'm Already There"
For no matter where I am, or where I go,
I am already there.
I promised, one day I would be home,
So I asked that you'd wait for me, I shouldn't be long.
Love, I am coming home, just a little late, so for me please be strong.
Will you meet me there at the unmarked gate?
Feel me right beside you, with arms tightly wrapped around you,
As the hearse comes into view.
Stay with me awhile my love, for there will be no tomorrow,
For this will be my last ride, our time for our last good-bye.
I promised, one day I would be with you forever,
Well my love now is my forever.
Just call my name and I'll be there.
I promise, I will dry your tears and ease your fears.
I promise, there will be a tomorrow, that will end your sad sorrow,
Be strong for me, until again we meet,
For then my love, we will join again, to share our love that will never end.

Walk Softly

Walk softly in theses old worn out shoes.
They have carried me many miles my life through.
Up and down the hills of heartache
All the days when I was blue.
They even carried me through a tear or two.
These old shoes are pretty worn and tired now
As I wipe my sweaty wrinkled brow.
A bit dusty from old dirt roads,
I have carried some pretty heavy loads.
Our Good Lord only knows,
But it's time now to pass them on,
To you my child, they'll be brand new,
So go ahead and slip 'um on.
They will go on and fit just right,
Not too snug nor too tight.
I pray that they give you wings to out run your fears.
Speed to out run your tears.
Give you comfort when things go bad.
A bounce to your step when you feel glad.
A spring to be ready to move ahead,
First thing in the morning, when you get out of bed.
They'll carry you through life's daily struggles,
And hold you up through life's uneasy juggles.
You'll know when it's time to pass them down,
When you step from this earths solid ground.
Where we'll meet again at Heaven's gate.
Where we'll watch from above in our brand new shoes,
The next generation to walk in those old worn out shoes.
So walk softly in my old shoes,
That I have passed down for you to use.
For they need to last until the end
When everyone is Home walking beside Jesus once again.

You Said You Would Come Back

I couldn't help but think of you first thing this morning.
I turned the radio on and they were playing our song.
I wish I could move past this emptiness you left behind,
But I just can't get you off my mind.
You have been gone for so long this time.
Do you even know I would welcome you home?
I just miss you and the life we had.
Do you ever even think of me?
Do you even remember we were starting a family?
Before you left that night, did it even cross your mind?
This life you were willing to leave behind.
Your friends haven't even heard from you,
Is this something maybe we can undo?
I'm tired of crying, I'm tired of fighting, and I'm tired of shouldering all
this hurt inside.
When I go to bed at night, I pray to God to send you home
Are my prayers in vain, am I going insane?
I watch every car that pulls in the drive.
Always thinking today is the day my eyes again will shine
Please baby please give me a clue, I can't fight this anymore,
I don't even know where or how you are.
Do you even know our son's been born?
What do I tell him, why you are gone?
Don't you even want to know his name?
How long do you plan on playing this game?
It was just a fight, a misunderstanding,
I'm sorry I didn't stop you from leaving then.
But can't we just begin again?
You said you would come back,
But how long do you think I will wait?
It has been too long now, several months to this date.
I cannot do this to myself any longer,
For our son, I need to be a little stronger.
I know I need to say good-bye, but my heart will not lie....
I miss you and the life we had, but my tears now must subside.

Grandma's poem

Estes Park

Oh serene Estes Park
Overhead you flys a lark;
In your silent quietude,
Away from human multitude.
Ah, the tinkling of the mountain streams is near,
It seems to say there's nothing in God's rest to fear.
And near tall mountains lay, open to the human heart,
With outstretched arms, greeting all to Estes Park.

Grandma's poem

Colorado

Colorado is 'way out west;
It's the state we love best.
There's heaps of joy and fresh clean air,
There are hunting trips to catch wild bear.
We love our Colorado,
And the Denver Post,
We know an Eldorado,
Of it we like to boast.
We will boast this Eldorado,
"Tis a privilege to live in Colorado."

Golden, Colorado

G- *is for gateway to the mountains of the west*
O- *is for oldest town and the best*
L- *is for lookout and Pahaska's tepee*
D- *is for Denver, whose lights we can see*
E- *is for end of Billy Cody's trail*
N- *is for native pines, his requiem they wail*

Jennifer

As our hearts are breaking
and the tears keep falling,
we'll forever wonder...
Why the Lord came calling.
As we're all left here to wonder why,
the answers to the questions just go on by.
We'll never forget your greatest fight,
nor how you left us, that tragic night.
The memories you gave us,
since you were young
will have to sustain us,
for the years to come.
We're all gathered together
as our family unites,
to remember forever...
A smile...
A laugh...
A simple touch...
Even the sound of you voice
we'll miss so much!
Now it's time to say good-bye,
til we meet again in Heaven's light.
We'll wait patiently as time goes by
for us all to reunite.

Heavens Angel

You came to me on a sunny day,
Small and precious all the way.
I couldn't breath as fear raced inside,
something was wrong, they had you aside.
" Not breathing," I heard them say,
the room started spinning as they whisked you away.
Then you were transported that very same day,
to a new hospital far away.
When I seen you again, tubes were everywhere,
I had to catch my breath as I was unprepared.
My heart was breaking, my eyes held tears,
my body trembled with newfound fears.
You were not going to make it, I started to pray,
"Please God, don't let her suffer anymore this way".
You opened your eyes and looked up at me,
Forty days today, you have stayed with me.
You can go now and forever rest,
for the Angels are here to take the best.

Grandma's poem

Modern Wash Day

Mothers in the kitchen
Washing up the duds
Sisters in the pantry
Bottling up the suds
Fathers in the cellar
Mixing up the hops
Johnnies on the front porch
Watching for the cops

Listeners

Everybody's says it, nobody knows it.
Listeners hear no good of themselves.
Listen at the keyhole and you'll hear,
news of yourself.
Little pitchers have great ears.

"Way Out West in Kansas"

The bride (at telephone): Oh John, do come home!
I've mixed the plugs in some way.
The radio is all covered with frost,
And the electric ice-box is singing
"Way Out West in Kansas"

Grandma's poem

A Happy Eastertide

Morn's roseate hues have
Decked the sky
The Lord has risen with victory
Let earth be glad
And raise the cry
Halleluiah!

A Thoughtful Easter

Though many miles divide us,
My thoughts toward you do stray,
For I wish you peace and happiness
On this Joyous Easter Day.

Thank You

Thank you for the memories that you give to me,
as each day starts out new.
Thank you for the time you spend with me,
it lifts my every mood.

Thank you for understanding me,
in no matter what I do.
Thank you for your patience,
for all I put you through.

I hope that when you need me,
I'll be there for you.
I'll be the rock to lean on,
and tell your troubles to.

Learning How to Pray

Learning how to pray
Should not be hard to do
Should be easy, but I have strayed so far from You.
My apologies Dear Lord.
I will kneel down now, Bow my head, fold my hands in prayer,
and give to You,
my worries, my fears, and all my tears.
Yes, I feel it, a tear slides down my face, as I sit and spend a moment with You.
You have held me up too many times,
with me not even aware
of how many burdens you have lifted and carried away from me.
How weak I must be.
How many times have I felt You,
but have turned the other way,
when all You wanted was just to spend a few minutes of time with me, during my
busy day.
My heart feels heavy.
I know I have wronged You in many of my ways,
but now I am back, and to You I give Praise.
My eyes are clearer now, and forever You will be,
right beside me Lord, where You will always see, that
never shall I stray again,
never will I look the other way,
and never will I be lonely
because on You I can depend.

Baby Boy

Ten little fingers,
Ten little toes,
And very tiny button nose.
All wrapped up in a bundle of blue,
A baby boy to rock
And sing a lullaby to.
He is sent from the purest love,
From our gracious Lord up above.
He will give you such pleasure and such joy,
Oh, what a beautiful baby boy!
A reflection of mom,
A reflection of dad,
When you look into his eyes
You will see the love, which you two have.
When you snuggle him in your arms,
Say a word of thanks,
For he is your tiny bundle
Given to just to the two of you!

Secrets

Telling secrets in the night,
Hold me tender, close and tight.
Press your lips so soft and moist,
Against my check, I so enjoy.

Telling secrets in the night,
Let us love by the firelight.
Snuggle close til dawn does break,
Our emotions are not fake.

Telling secrets in the night,
Makes my life feel so bright.
Moonlight strolls along the beach,
With kisses tasting like a peach.

Telling secrets in the night,
My heart feels so light.
Whisper you love me in my ear,
For if you do, I'll know no fear.

You Were Always There

You looked so sad today,
Not a smile upon your face.
I saw what looked like a tear,
As you came by me so near.

I know I've hurt you in such a way,
How could I expect you to ever stay.
I was so wrong to do what I did,
But oh how you loved me as you always did.

I was unfaithful while you were away,
But you kept calling, begging me to stay.
You never gave up tho times were rough,
I owe you so much. How can I give enough.

We came along way,
But we're back together to stay.
With prayer, talking, and loving to,
We will see each other through.

Grandma's poem

The New Year

There's a New Year coming, coming
Out of some beautiful sphere,
His baby eyes are bright,
With hope and delight,
We welcome you, Happy New Year.

There's an Old Year going, going
Away in the winter dear,
His beard is like snow
And his footsteps are slow.
Good-bye to you, weary Old Year.

There's always a New Year coming,
There is always an Old Year to go,
And never a tear, drops the Happy New Year,
As he scatters his gifts in the snow.

Talking Eyes

You say my eyes talk,
Do you know what they say?
Could your eyes also,
Be talking in such away?
I see a story within your eyes.
Am I to hope they say the same as mine.
Could your eyes be talking,
But really it's a lie?
You know the story within my eyes.
You see it there each and every day.
Would you please tell me in a simple way,
What your eyes might be saying, from day to day.
How long must I wait.
Can you not see my heartache?
Come away with me to spend a day,
You'll not regret our time of play.
Stop this foolish pride of yours,
Let it go today.
Come to me and tell me truth,
what really do you hide
within your talking eyes.

A Mother's Day Prayer

A Mother's day prayer is exactly what I'll do.
I'll pray for you, Mother, as each day starts anew.
As the sun arises in the sky, so very deep in blue,
Know that I am thinking, very sweetly of you.
I'll pray for your safety in each step you take.
In God's love shall you never forsake.
May He hold your hand in stumbles, in which you might make,
And know that He forgives you for any of your mistakes.
I'll pray for you Mother, that you may be strong.
In a day's many struggles, that you may carry on.
In your heart of many burdens, I give to you a song,
And know in your heart, you could never do me wrong.
I will send to you... a whisper in the wind,
To let you know I love you, and that will never end.
Know that my arms, are wrapped around you,
This Mother's Day year, for you my Mother, are so very dear.
I'll pray that as the moon casts it's midnight glow,
You will feel my love for you, continue to grow.
As you lay to rest your weary head, have sweet dreams,
And do not dread,
For I am always with you, no matter where you go,
For I am part of you, and that will always be so.

Winter

Another winter has come to stay.
Another winter come what may.
Snowflakes falling to the ground,
Not making any noticeable sounds.

White and beautiful as they may be,
I wish the summer sun I would see.
More snowflakes falling all around,
Somehow does make a beautiful background.

I feel the cold of yet, another winter,
It's bite is cold and very bitter.
This is it, I need to feel better,
I need to end my winter anger.

I will accept it for I cannot change it,
I will just have to outwit it.
So in the snow I go,
And snowballs I will throw!

Friendship of the heart

Have you ever met someone who became a friend?
One who has touched your very heart?
One you have never laid your eyes upon,
However, knew it was friendship from the start.

Even though you might be miles apart,
Whom may never even meet face to face?
Be sure to share what God lends to you,
A friendship to share your life through.

Weather it may be a Christmas card you send.
A phone call every now and then,
Maybe an e-mail a few times a week,
Doesn't that still make your friendship unique?

Somewhere out there, is one in need,
Of a friendship from you, or maybe me.
You never know how two hearts often meet,
However, when they do, it becomes complete.

Troubles

It's always greener on the other side,
When life's troubles pass you by.
First your up, then your down,
Always spinning round and round.

What may come, you never know,
You may just have to let it go.
To some it's good, to others it's bad,
Just remember what you have.

One day it might be bleak,
The next could be at it's peak.
Don't give up when it's rough,
Just hang in there and stay tough.

In times of pain and sorrow,
There is always a new tomorrow.
So remember and believe,
Life is precious to you and to me.

In the Dark

What has become of us?
We are strangers in the dark.
Things we once did,
We now do apart.
Dreams we once shared,
They are no longer there.
Our future looks glim,
For we no longer care.
Ghosts from our past,
Makes our lives blur by.
Our loves no longer there,
For us to even care.
What should we do?
What can we do?
Is this a hopeless situation,
That neither of us will try to mend.

Your Gone

I hear the thunder all around,
As I lie here in our bed.
Another sleepless night awaits me,
As thoughts of you go through my head.
It's so lonely since you've been gone,
I hear nothing but sadness in these 'ol country songs.
I look at your picture...and still I wonder why.
I can't believe you left me.
I feel like I could die.
I wait by the phone...
All day...
All night.
Why don't you call me? Why can't we make things right?
Tomorrow, I will accept that you are gone.
I will turn off the radio...
No more listening to sad country songs.

Grandma's poem

Untitled

Whether I live or whether I die,
Whatever the worlds I see-
I shall come to you bye and bye
And you will come to me.

Whoever was foolish, we were wise,
We crossed the boundary line.
I saw my soul look out of your eyes.
You saw your soul in mine.